For Liz

Pete and Polo's
Big School Adventure

Adrian Reynolds

Orchard Books • New York

Orchard Books, A Grolier Company, 95 Madison Avenue, New York, NY 10016

Manufactured in Hong Kong/China
The text of this book is set in 18 point Plantin. The illustrations are watercolor.
1 3 5 7 9 10 8 6 4 2

Library of Congress Cataloging-in-Publication Data
Reynolds, Adrian. [Pete and Polo's nursery school adventure]
Pete and Polo's big school adventure / by Adrian Reynolds.—1st American ed.   p.   cm.
First published in Great Britain under the title: Pete and Polo's nursery school adventure
Summary: Pete and his polar bear are both nervous on their first day of school, especially when Polo
finds he is the only bear that's not brown.
ISBN 0-531-30275-X
[1. First day of school—Fiction. 2. Schools—Fiction. 3. Polar bear—Fiction. 4. Toys—Fiction.] I. Title.
PZ7.R33215 Pe 2000   [E]—dc21   99-51523

"Wake up, Polo," said Pete. Today was their first day at school on their own—without Mom. But Polo thought he'd stay in bed.

At breakfast Pete whispered to Polo,
"This is going to be our best adventure yet."

Polo wasn't so sure. "I don't think polar bears normally go to school," he said in a wobbly voice.

When they arrived at school, there were lots of moms and dads and children. It was very noisy. All the other children had brought their teddy bears too.

Ms. Rose was waiting at the door to greet them.

"Hello, Pete," she said. "This is Henry. Today is his first day at school on his own too."

Ms. Rose took them inside and helped them hang up their coats and bags. Pete had his own special peg. So did Henry.

Pete took Polo out of his bag.

"Your bear's a funny color," said Henry. "Why isn't he brown like mine?"

"I'm not a funny color," said Polo with a sniff.

"He's a polar bear," said Pete. "He's supposed to be white."

"Follow me," said Ms. Rose as she led Pete and Polo into a big room full of children. It was full of bears too, but they were *all* brown. Pete squeezed Polo's paw very tightly.

Ms. Rose showed Pete and Polo
the painting corner . . .

and then they built towers out
of building blocks.

They sailed boats in
the water . . .

and played dress-up.

There was even a pet corner. Pete fed the rabbit . . .

and Polo fed the goldfish.
"They're saying hello
to me," said Polo, feeling
a little less sniffly.

Soon it was story time. Ms. Rose read a story about a king and queen and their pet dragon. Some of the other bears joined in, making loud, growly dragon noises. Polo sat very quietly and very close to Pete.

Grrrr!

Grrrr!

Grrrr!

Grrrr!

Grrrr!

After the story, they had milk and apples.

Ms. Rose took some of the children over to the sinks to wash their hands.

"Look, Polo," said Pete. "They're just the right size for us."

At recess all the children went outside, leaving their bears safely behind. Pete hoped Polo wouldn't be too lonely.

But he threw the ball around with the other children, and together they all made lots of noise.

Soon it was time to go back inside—but at the doorway the children stopped suddenly. There, in the corner, was an enormous pile of teddy bears. How would they ever be able to tell whose was whose?

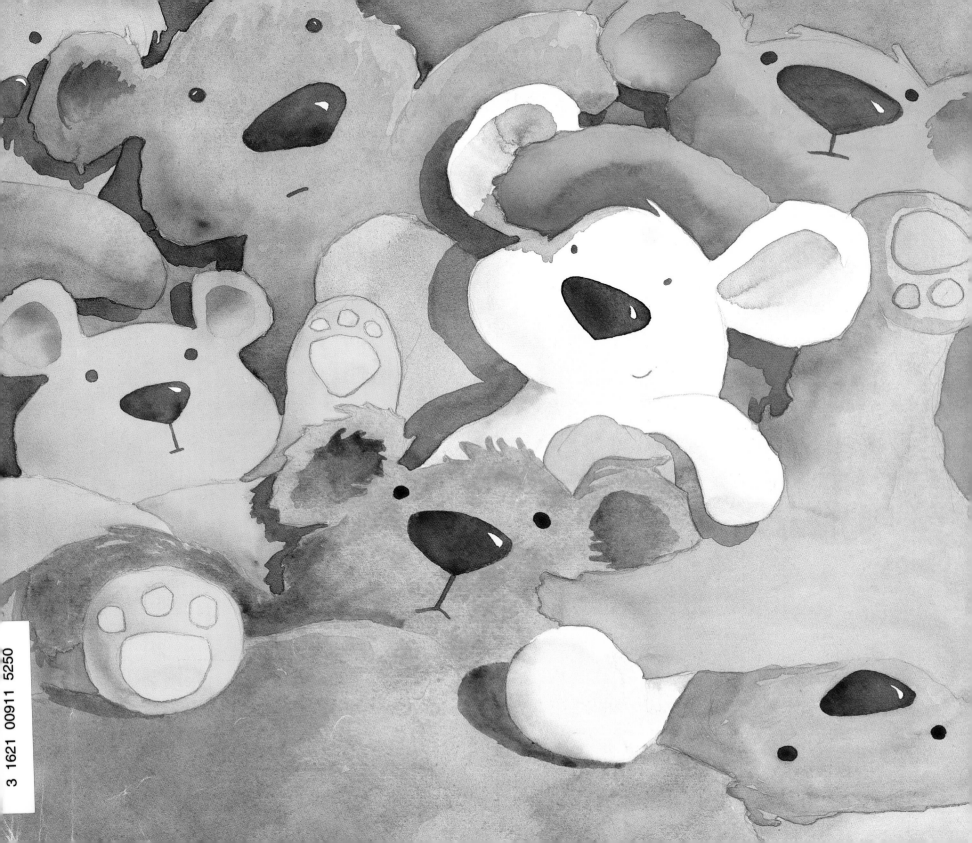

"Polo!" said Pete, spotting his own very special friend right away and giving him a great big hug.

Polo was looking smiley for the first time all day. "I had a lovely time with all the other bears," he said.

When school was over, Pete and Polo rushed outside to where
Mom was waiting. They had so much to tell her . . .

. . . and they both agreed
that going to school was
their best adventure yet.